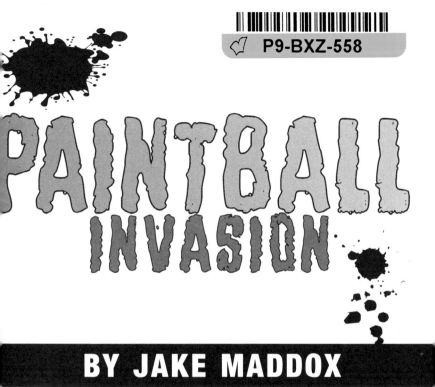

PAINTBALL INVASION

BY JAKE MADDOX

illustrated by Sean Tiffany

text by Bob Temple

Librarian Reviewer
Chris Kreie
Media Specialist, Eden Prairie Schools, MN
MS in Information Media, St. Cloud State University, MN

Reading Consultant
Mary Evenson
Middle School Teacher, Edina Public Schools, MN
MA in Education, University of Minnesota

STONE ARCH BOOKS
Minneapolis San Diego

Impact Books are published by Stone Arch Books
A Capstone Imprint
151 Good Counsel Drive, P.O. Box 669
Mankato, Minnesota 56002
www.capstonepub.com

Library of Congress Cataloging-in-Publication Data
Maddox, Jake.
    Paintball Invasion / by Jake Maddox; illustrated by Sean Tiffany.
    p. cm. — (Impact Books — A Jake Maddox Sports Story)
    ISBN 978-1-4342-0466-0 (library binding)
    ISBN 978-1-4342-0516-2 (paperback)
    [1. Paintball (Game)—Fiction. 2. Sportsmanship—Fiction.]
I. Tiffany, Sean, ill. II. Title.
PZ7.M25643Pii 2008
[Fic]—dc22   2007031258

Summary: Josh and Chad have been using the same place as a paintball
field forever. But during one game, something weird happens. As the
guys are marked, they realize they haven't been marked by the opposing
team. Instead, someone new is attacking them. Someone unknown. Will
they discover who's out to stop their paintballing fun? It's going to take
all their skills and teamwork to stop the sinister invasion.

Creative Director: Heather Kindseth
Senior Graphic Designer: Kay Fraser

Printed in the United States of America in Stevens Point, Wisconsin.
102009
005625R

TABLE OF CONTENTS

CHAPTER 1

MARKED

I heard the whiz of the paintball go past my ear.

Splat! It smashed against the bark of the huge oak tree I was hiding behind.

I wasn't doing a very good job of hiding. The paintball almost hit me right in the head.

I couldn't see the person who had tried to mark me. Quickly, I dove behind a bush.

I could feel my heart pounding in my chest. Before I could do anything, though, I needed to check to make sure I wasn't out of the game. If I'd been hit, that was it for me.

I didn't think that the paintball had hit me. But in other games, I'd been marked without knowing it. Sometimes, if a paintball hit my helmet, I wouldn't feel it. Then I'd be out of the game.

There was only one way to find out. I had to get to a safe place. I needed to be able to take my helmet off. I didn't really feel safe where I was, hidden behind the bush. That last shot had surprised me, because I thought I knew exactly where my opponents were.

My best friend, Chad, and I were the last two members of our team still in the game.

The other team was down to two players too. Chad and I had been signaling to each other, and we thought we had trapped those two players between us. We figured we just needed to keep watch, and one of them would move, giving us a shot.

But the shot that had almost marked me had come from behind me. There was almost no way that one of the other players had snuck out from between us without me seeing him.

So how had it happened?

I thought hard, trying to figure out what had happened. I was pretty sure I'd been paying close attention. And I was also pretty sure that there were only two players left on their team, and they were somewhere in front of me.

It didn't make sense. But there was something more important that I needed to worry about. I needed to find out if I was still in the game. I had to check my helmet.

Crawling on the ground as quietly as I could, I started to move toward our hideout.

Last summer, Chad and I had built a little fort between two bushes. We used a bunch of old wood that we found by the side of a road. We painted the fort in camouflage colors, so no one could see it.

It was a great place to hide during paintball games. We could stay safe there and make plans.

We made a promise never to fire a shot out of there. We didn't want anyone else to know where it was.

We were pretty sure that no one had ever found our fort. After all, every time we went to the fort, it was empty. If someone else had found it, they definitely would have tried to use it as a hideout during a paintball game.

As I crawled toward the hideout, I stayed as low to the ground as I could.

After a few minutes, I was about 50 feet away from the hideout. I started crawling faster.

I could see the little wood fort, and if I could get there, I'd be safe.

That's when I felt it. *Splat!* Something hit my leg, hard.

It stung sharply for a second. The pain went away quickly, but my anger bubbled as I realized what had happened.

I didn't want to look down at my pants, but I did. There, right on the side of my left leg, was the yellow blob of a paintball splotch.

Just like that, I was out of the game.

CHAPTER 2

YELLOW?

The only good thing about getting hit was that I hadn't made it to the hideout.

Whoever marked me was watching me. If they had waited longer to shoot, they might have seen me go into the hideout. Then our secret fort wouldn't be a secret anymore.

All I could do now was stand up. I had to tell everyone that I'd been marked.

The helmet marking, if it had happened, didn't matter anymore. Now I was out of the game for sure.

I stood up and raised my hands to show that I was leaving the playing area. Then I had to let Chad know what had happened.

"I'm out!" I yelled. "Chad, you're on your own."

Chad didn't say anything, of course. He didn't want to give away his position.

Even though my team was down to just one player, we weren't out of the game. Chad was still safe. He was one of the best and smartest paintball players around.

I remembered other games, when he'd been the last player left on our team. He'd still been able to mark three or four players on the other team to get us the win.

I couldn't do anything anymore, though. According to the rules we use, players who are out of the game can't do anything to help players who are still alive. I couldn't even signal to Chad.

So I just walked back to the starting point. I'd wait there for the game to end.

When I got to the starting point, I saw that players from both teams were standing around. A couple of guys had climbed trees to try to get a good look at what was going on. Most of the guys were just hanging out, talking.

There were six guys there, three from each team. We had started with five players on a side. The players were all kids from our middle school. We were all friends, and we played paintball almost every weekend.

Each time, we chose teams by picking bandanas out of a bag. We'd put an equal number of red and blue bandanas in the bag.

Then we'd reach in without looking, and whichever color bandana we pulled, that's the team we were on. That would be the color of the paintballs that we'd shoot, too.

When I got back to the starting point, I noticed something weird. The other three guys on my team, the blue team, had all been marked by red paintballs. The guys on the red team were all marked with bright blue paint, the color my team was using.

But the splotch on my leg was yellow!

"Hey, guys," I said. "Who's shooting yellow?"

"What do you mean, Josh?" asked James, one of the guys on the other team. "We're shooting red, remember?"

"Yeah, I know," I said. "But I got marked with yellow."

Just then, Chad came walking out of the woods. He had a bright yellow splotch on his chest. When he got up to us, he noticed right away that he and I were the only ones marked with yellow.

"All right," he said. "What's going on here?"

CHAPTER 3

SOMETHING WEIRD

The eight of us just stared at each other. No one knew what was going on or what to say.

Finally, James looked over at me. "I think I know what's going on, guys," he said. "Michael's got a big box of yellow paintballs at his house. Maybe he ran out of the red ones we were supposed to be using and just started using his yellow ones."

That made sense to me. It didn't explain how I got confused about where their team's players were. But it did explain the yellow splotches on Chad and me.

James called out to his teammates. "Michael! Ray! The game is over. We won, so you can come back to the start!" he yelled.

There was a really long pause, but no noise from the woods.

Then we all started screaming. "Game's over!" we called. "Red wins! Michael, Ray, come on in."

Finally, there was a little rustling in the woods. At last, we saw Ray walking down the path. He was holding his marker over his head. That meant that he was out of the game.

As soon as he turned the corner on the path and could see us, Ray put his arms down. His head drooped too.

I could tell that he thought he was out of the game.

No one said a word as Ray got closer. Finally, when he was within shouting distance, Ray called out, "Sorry, guys. I got hit."

"When?" James asked. I realized that he wanted to know if it was before or after Chad and I had been hit.

"It was just a second ago," Ray said. "You know the rules. We have to leave the field as soon as we get hit."

Now we were all confused. If all five players on the blue team were out, how had Ray gotten hit?

"Ray, there wasn't anybody left on the other team to mark you," James said.

Ray frowned. "Well, I don't know how that's possible," he said. "I have the mark on my back to prove it."

James grabbed Ray's shoulder and swung him around. There, plain as the sun in the sky, was a big yellow splotch on the middle of Ray's back.

We were all stunned. Finally, James looked around at the rest of us. "Okay," he said, "now this is just plain weird."

CHAPTER 4

GONE CRAZY

"What's everyone looking at?" Ray asked. "Something wrong with my back?"

"It's yellow," I said. "The paintball you got hit with. It was yellow."

"Yellow?" Ray asked. He sounded confused.

Suddenly, he noticed the yellow splat on my leg and the one on Chad's chest. "Wait a second," he said. "What is going on around here?"

"That's what we're trying to figure out," said James. "Somebody's using yellow paintballs. At first, we thought it was Michael, getting rid of some of his paintballs. But if he's marking his own teammates, then he's gone crazy."

I thought about it. Michael was a little bit odd. He had a weird sense of humor and he got bored really easily. So it wouldn't be all that surprising if he just got bored playing the game the normal way and decided to start marking everyone with the wrong color, just for fun.

"It's got to be Michael," I said. "He's just messing with us."

Chad laughed. "That's probably it," he said. "I wonder if he knows that everybody's out."

"Why?" James asked. "Do you have something in mind?"

"Oh, yeah, you know I do," Chad said.

Chad had some kind of plan brewing. I could tell. He smiled at me. Then he explained his plan to us.

Between Ray, who was Michael's teammate, and me and Chad, we thought we could figure out where Michael was. Chad and I knew where he'd been when we left the field. And Ray knew where Michael had been when Ray got marked.

Chad's idea was that all nine of the other players, no matter which team they were on, would spread out in a circle around that spot. Then we'd slowly close in on Michael. We'd all mark him with paintballs when we found him.

It was a great plan. We all agreed to it. Then we headed back into the woods, in different directions.

Chad figured out how to tell us what to do without letting Michael know. He said he'd make a bird call when it was time for all of us to head toward the spot where we thought Michael was hiding.

A few minutes later, I heard Chad's bird call. Then I started marching slowly in.

Creeping, crawling, and moving along as quietly as possible, our circle kept getting smaller and smaller. Finally, we were within about 30 yards of each other.

I could see all eight of the other guys. James thought he spotted Michael, and he signaled the location to all of us with his hands.

We all nodded. Then we headed to the spot.

There were a bunch of shrubs in the area, but there was one pile of sticks that looked like someone had made it. Michael had to be hidden under there.

Finally, we were within about ten yards of the pile of sticks. James held up three fingers, telling us that we'd pounce on the count of three. He signaled to Chad to pull the sticks aside. The rest of us would get Michael.

I was pumped. This was our big chance to get back at Michael for messing with our game. We knew the ambush of paintballs wouldn't hurt him, but it was sure to surprise him. It would be pretty funny at the same time.

James counted to three with his fingers. Then Chad ran for the stick pile, and the rest of us closed in.

Chad dove onto the pile, knocking sticks in all directions. As they flew off and Chad rolled away, the other eight of us all opened fire on the spot.

But after a second or two, we all stopped. Our paintballs were hitting empty ground.

Michael wasn't there.

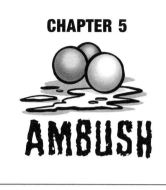

CHAPTER 5

AMBUSH

When we figured out that Michael was still missing, none of us really knew what to do next. We all stared at the ground. No one moved or said a word. We were all in shock.

After all, we had been so sure that Michael was there. But we couldn't see him anywhere. We had been wrong about his location.

What were we supposed to do now?

Finally, Chad broke the silence with his laughter. But it wasn't happy laughter, like someone had just told a joke. It was weird, crazy laughter.

Chad stopped laughing. Then he said, "I don't know where he is, but when I find him, I'm going to—"

"Find who?" came a voice from behind us. It was Michael!

We all spun around and pointed our markers at him. But when we saw him, none of us tried to mark him.

Michael looked a little scared. And his shirt and pants were covered with yellow splotches.

"Guys," he mumbled, "I got ambushed. And I never saw the guy coming. It was like he was everywhere, all around me."

We all lowered our markers. Chad did too, but I could tell that he didn't believe a word of Michael's story.

"Oh, please," Chad said. "You probably overheard us and splattered yourself with yellow paint. You're just crazy enough."

"I'm not crazy," Michael said. "Why would I shoot myself with a color we're not even using? That doesn't make any sense, Chad."

Chad snatched Michael's marker out of his hand. He examined it closely.

It was full of red paintballs, and it didn't have any yellow spots on it at all. Chad's theory was starting to come apart.

"Come on, Michael," Chad said. "Where's the marker you were using for the yellow balls?"

"What are you talking about?" Michael yelled back. "Are you crazy? I wasn't the one using yellow balls!"

There was dead silence. I was worried. I started to think that there might be a fight.

"I'm telling you, I got ambushed," Michael said finally. "They were all over the place."

I could tell that some of the other guys believed Michael. I looked closely at his face. He really did look scared. I was starting to believe him too.

Then a *whizz* went through the group. It came in from my left and sped quickly past my ear.

Then came a call from my right. "Caw-caw!" That was followed by a storm of yellow paintballs.

The paintballs were coming in from all directions. We ran, but it quickly became clear there was no way to escape.

We fired off a few weak shots, but there wasn't much hope. The yellow paintballs just kept raining down on us.

Where were the people who were marking us? There had to be lots of them.

Finally, with another call of "Caw-caw!" the attack ended as fast as it had started.

As we lay on the floor of the woods, our clothes covered with yellow splotches, a stranger walked into the middle of our group.

CHAPTER 6

BANNED

The guy was dressed all in black. He was wearing black shoes, black pants, a black long-sleeved shirt, and a black helmet.

He was even wearing a black mask. The mask covered up his face. I couldn't tell who he was.

I was pretty sure, though, that the guy was older than us. I thought he was probably in high school.

He turned and looked at each of us.

"This is a warning," he said. "These woods belong to us. Come back again, and the same thing will happen to you."

James sat up straight. "Wait a second. You can't just make us leave these woods," he said. "We've been playing here forever. And the woods don't belong to you."

"You don't play here anymore," the guy in black said. "The kiddie games are done. Time for the big kids to play."

He turned and started to walk away. He wasn't in any hurry. I could tell that he wanted to make a big exit, like something from the movies.

Chad scrambled to his knees. He drew his marker up to his eye.

"I wouldn't do that, if I were you," the stranger said.

He didn't turn. He just kept walking away.

Chad slowly lowered the marker as the figure disappeared into the woods. We each struggled to get back to our feet.

Getting hit by a paintball doesn't really cause any damage, but it does sting for a little while. We were all rubbing the spots where we got marked.

"Do you believe me now, Chad?" Michael asked quietly. "Still think I'm shooting myself?"

Chad shook his head. "No. I'm sorry," he said.

The mystery of the yellow paintballs was solved. But we were still left with one question.

What should we do next?

The ten of us decided to have a meeting, right there in the woods. We sat in a circle to talk.

Some of the guys were scared. The ambushers were older, and they wanted the woods. The guys who were scared thought we should find another place to hang out.

Other guys thought maybe we could talk to the older guys. We could agree to play at different times.

Then there were a few of us who thought there was no reason to give anything up. Those guys wanted to battle it out with the older guys for the rights to the woods.

We weren't coming to an agreement at all. I didn't even know what I thought we should do. We sat in the middle of the woods and stared at each other.

Finally, Chad spoke up. He sounded like the voice of reason.

"Look, those were high school guys," he said. "They aren't going to play paintball every weekend like we do. I think they were just messing with us. They got their kicks by scaring us, and now they are probably done. I bet if we come back next week, they won't even be here."

After we all thought about it, everyone seemed to agree that Chad was right. The older guys didn't really care about the woods at all. They just wanted to scare us. With that settled, we all slapped hands and said our goodbyes and headed for home.

As Chad and I walked out of the woods, we were able to laugh about the guy in black. We started to make plans for the following weekend.

Then we walked past our hidden fort in the woods. My heart sank.

There, in bright yellow paint, on a side of the hideout that used to be hidden, were these words:

WE FOUND IT!

CHAPTER 7

TRYING AGAIN

Our secret fort wasn't a secret anymore. But Chad and I still decided to head back to the woods the next Saturday.

We decided that if we didn't show up, it would seem like we were giving up. We wanted the older guys to know that we were serious.

So on Saturday, we walked together to the woods. There we were, right at the usual meeting place at the usual time.

At first, it was just Chad and me. We wondered if the other guys had chickened out.

Slowly but surely, however, they started to show up. James was next, and a few minutes later, Michael and Ray showed up together.

Three more of our friends walked down the path a few minutes later, giving us a total of eight. We waited a while to see if anyone else would show. Finally, we decided just to play with eight guys.

We threw eight bandanas into a bag, four red and four blue. Then we turned our backs to the bag, reached in one at a time, and each pulled one out.

Chad and I were the first two. We both pulled blue.

I breathed a sign of relief. It was always more fun when we were on the same team.

Then we set up the rules for the day. Each team would head off in different directions, and take 10 minutes to make a plan. Then the game would start at exactly 12:30.

We made sure all of our watches had the same time. Then we headed off.

We had each walked about five steps in different directions when the attack began. They fired and fired.

We were all out in the open on the path. That meant that we were easy to mark.

I dove for the bushes, but it was no use. I was marked right away. In about a minute, we were all lying on the ground, curled up like little balls.

The leader of the guys in black yelled a warning. "Get up and get out of here," he yelled. "These woods are ours."

We did as we were told. That was the end of paintball that weekend.

CHAPTER 8

JUST US

After the ambush, Chad and I talked about it. We still believed that older guys would have better things to do than paintball every weekend.

So we went back the next week, and the week after that. Each week, we returned to the woods to try to have a game.

Each week, we were ambushed again. And each week, the number of players for our game got smaller.

Finally, one Saturday, it was just Chad and me. Before the ambush started, he looked at me and said, "Josh, I'm tired of this. Let's just get out of here."

It was the first time I ever saw Chad look nervous. But his nervousness didn't last long. I could tell that he was beginning to come up with a plan.

That night, sitting on the front steps of my house, Chad told me about his idea.

CHAPTER 9

CHAD'S PLAN

Chad had figured out a way to fight back. We knew that it might not get our woods back, but it was a step in the right direction.

The first step was to get some of the guys who usually played with us to help.

That was pretty easy. We talked to all of them at school. Six guys agreed to meet at my house with all their paintball gear at nine o'clock on Saturday morning.

Chad and I had figured everything out in advance. The key to the plan was surprising the older guys. To really surprise them, our ambush had to be different from when they ambushed us.

Also, we had to be spread out all around the woods. That meant each of us would have a good chance of marking one of the older guys.

"Basically, what we're playing is the paintball game to end all paintball games," Chad explained. "They have a huge advantage, because they are older than we are. But we have one big thing on our side. We're the only ones who know we're playing!"

All our friends laughed. Chad and I explained to each guy where to go, and what his job was.

This was no ordinary ambush. We were going to surprise the high school guys in a way no one had done in any of our games before.

Around 10 o'clock on Saturday morning, we all headed out to the woods.

Each of us was carrying two markers. We were also wearing camouflage clothes so we'd blend into the woods.

Chad wanted us to get to the woods early. That would give us plenty of time to get into our positions.

Then we'd have to stay perfectly still until the older kids showed up to play.

The biggest secret was that we'd be climbing into the trees. The older guys wouldn't expect to be ambushed from above. They'd expect it from ground level.

As long as we didn't give away our positions, we'd be in the perfect spot to really get them.

Right on cue, the older guys starting showing up at noon.

After about 15 minutes, they had all arrived. Then they chose their teams and were off to start their planning.

"All right, guys," their leader said. "Let's have a good clean game today. At least we don't have to get rid of those little kids." I tried really hard not to laugh.

We could have ambushed them all at once, but Chad had other ideas. He wanted to wait until they were all spread out.

That way, none of them would be able to know exactly what was happening. No one could warn the others.

So far, everything was working perfectly.

None of them saw any of us. They were in the middle of preparing for their game. They all thought that they had the woods to themselves.

At exactly 12:30, our attack began.

CHAPTER 10

THE
BATTLE

There was a player on the blue team in clear view. Chad fired his marker.

Splat!

The guy was marked in the back of the leg with a bright red blob. "Aw, man!" the player yelled.

He stood up right away. Then he held his marker over his head, showing that he was out.

The guy looked pretty mad that he had been marked. He slowly walked back to the starting point.

Across the clearing, Chad nodded at me. That meant it was my turn. I raised my marker so that I was ready. Then I looked around for a player. After a few minutes, a red-team player walked right past me.

I easily marked him with a blue paintball. He stood up. Then he held up his arms and declared himself out of the game, just like the first player had.

The plan was to mark everyone on the red team. Then we'd mark at least a couple of the guys on the blue team.

The guy who'd ambushed us seemed to be the leader of the older guys. He was on the blue team.

We wouldn't mark him. Not yet, anyway.

Soon, everyone on the red team would be out. Then the blue team would think they had won. That's when we'd ambush whoever was left on the field.

If our plan went the way we wanted it to, one of the people left on the field would include the leader. He would be ambushed with the rest of them.

A couple of players called themselves out. Then the rest of the guys in our group knew the plan had been launched perfectly. They all picked out the nearest older guy and marked him with ease.

We were each careful to use the right marker every time. We'd brought two, after all. That was part of Chad's plan.

If we were marking a person on the blue team, we'd use the marker that had red paintballs. And if we were marking a red player, we'd use blue paintballs. We had to use the right colors to make the players think they were being marked by their opponents, not us.

We had one other advantage: We were in the trees! The players were easy targets from above. Also, we could easily spot them from our perches in the branches.

Finally, only two players were left. They were both on the blue team. One of them was the guy who'd ambushed us in the woods.

Neither of the guys knew that their teammates and opponents were all gone. They hadn't figured that out yet.

The guys were right in the center of the woods. My friends and I all climbed down from the trees.

We surrounded the older guys. We would wait for the right time to attack.

We had to be ready. Once it was time, we needed to move quickly.

When the last player who'd been marked got back to the starting point, the older guys would all start calling to these two guys to tell them that the blue team had won.

Quietly, we waited for the call.

Finally, someone yelled from the starting point. "Hey, Bill! Harry! You can come in now. We won!"

The two guys stood up straight and yelled in victory.

We stood up straight, too, and marked them both from six different directions.

"Yeah!" Chad screamed. He gave me a high five. We were all jumping for joy.

The rest of the older guys came running when they heard the yelling. When they got a look at Harry and Bill, they all started laughing.

"Hey, nice work, guys!" one of them said. "You beat us at our own game!"

"I told you we should have just joined their game instead of scaring them away," another one of the older guys said. "These kids are good players."

Suddenly, I got nervous. The leader of the older guys looked really mad and embarrassed. He frowned and looked at his friends, and then looked over at us.

Chad and I looked at each other. Chad frowned. He seemed worried.

After a few seconds, the older guy shook his head and laughed. "Fine, they can play," he said. Then he pointed at Chad and me and added, "As long as these two guys are on my team."

ABOUT THE AUTHOR

Bob Temple lives in Rosemount, Minnesota, with his wife and three children. He has written more than thirty books for children. Over the years, he has coached more than twenty kids' soccer, basketball, and baseball teams. He also loves visiting classrooms to talk about his writing.

ABOUT THE ILLUSTRATOR

When Sean Tiffany was growing up, he lived on a small island off the coast of Maine. Every day, from sixth grade until he graduated from high school, he had to take a boat to get to school. When Sean isn't working on his art, he works on a multimedia project called "OilCan Drive," which combines music and art. He has a pet cactus named Jim.

GLOSSARY

advantage (ad-VAN-tij)—something that helps you or is useful to you

ambush (AM-bush)—to hide and then attack

attention (uh-TEN-shuhn)—if you pay attention, you concentrate on something

camouflage (KAM-uh-flahzh)—covering that makes people blend in with their surroundings

damage (DAM-ij)—harm or serious hurt

fort (FORT)—a building that was built to be strong during attacks

hideout (HIDE-out)—a place where someone can hide

invasion (in-VAY-zhuhn)—an unwelcome entrance into someone else's territory

mark (MARK)—to hit with a paintball

marker (MARK-ur)—the piece of equipment used to shoot a paintball

opponent (uh-POH-nuhnt)—someone who is against you

signal (SIG-nuhl)—send a message or warning

splotch (SPLAHCH)—a marking

KEEPING PAINTBALL

Paintball is a very fun sport, but no sport is fun if someone gets hurt.

The best way to enjoy paintball is to play it safely.

Here are some tips from paintball experts that will help you enjoy the game.

Never point your marker at anyone or anything as a joke, or in a careless way.

Keep your "safety" on until it's time for the game to start.

To store your paintball marker, use a barrel plug and remove the CO_2 tank.

Never look down the barrel of your marker, even if it's not loaded

SAFE AND FUN

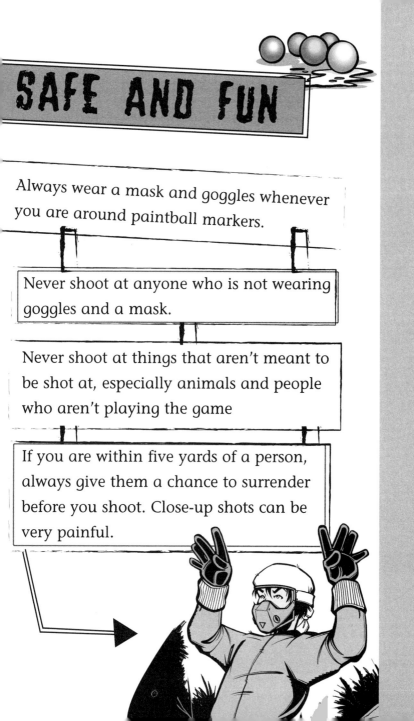

Always wear a mask and goggles whenever you are around paintball markers.

Never shoot at anyone who is not wearing goggles and a mask.

Never shoot at things that aren't meant to be shot at, especially animals and people who aren't playing the game

If you are within five yards of a person, always give them a chance to surrender before you shoot. Close-up shots can be very painful.

DISCUSSION QUESTIONS

1. Why didn't the older guys want to let the younger guys use the woods for paintball?

2. Some people think that paintball is a violent sport. What do you think? Explain your thoughts.

3. The younger guys choose to prove to the older guys that they should all be able to play paintball in the same area. What else could they have done?

WRITING PROMPTS

1. Do you have a group of people who you play a sport with on the weekend? Write a description of your group. What do you do? What do you like about it?

2. Have you ever thought that someone was treating you differently because of your age? How did you feel when that happened? What did you do? What are some other things you could have done?

3. Sometimes it's interesting to think about a story from someone else's point of view. Try writing the last chapter from the point of view of the older guys' leader. What does he think about? What does he see? How does he feel? Write it all down!

Anton loves playing football until Malik, the talented quarterback, starts acting strange. Instead of working with the team, Malik is just showing off. Anton has to fix the problem fast, before the quarterback ruins everything!

BY JAKE MADDOX

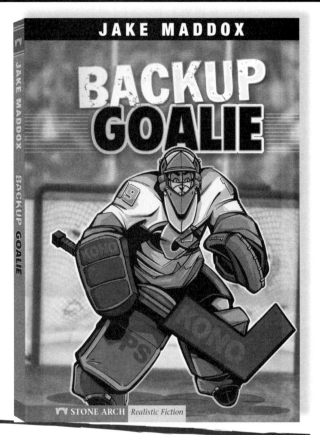

STONE ARCH *Realistic Fiction*

Jamie thought everything was perfect on his
hockey team. But when the goalie is injured,
Jamie has to step in to the unfamiliar position.
Can Jamie help his team skate to victory, or are
they on thin ice?

INTERNET SITES

Do you want to know more about subjects related to this book? Or are you interested in learning about other topics? Then check out FactHound, a fun, easy way to find Internet sites.

Our investigative staff has already sniffed out great sites for you!

Here's how to use FactHound:

1. Visit *www.facthound.com*

2. Select your grade level.

3. To learn more about subjects related to this book, type in the book's ISBN number: **9781434204660**.

4. Click the **Fetch It** button.

FactHound will fetch the best Internet sites for you!